THE WORLD WHICH SHALL BE FEARED

VISHAL DIXIT

Copyright © Vishal Dixit
All Rights Reserved.

This book has been published with all efforts taken to make the material error-free after the consent of the author. However, the author and the publisher do not assume and hereby disclaim any liability to any party for any loss, damage, or disruption caused by errors or omissions, whether such errors or omissions result from negligence, accident, or any other cause.

While every effort has been made to avoid any mistake or omission, this publication is being sold on the condition and understanding that neither the author nor the publishers or printers would be liable in any manner to any person by reason of any mistake or omission in this publication or for any action taken or omitted to be taken or advice rendered or accepted on the basis of this work. For any defect in printing or binding the publishers will be liable only to replace the defective copy by another copy of this work then available.

Contents

Disclaimer

This is a work of fiction. Unless otherwise indicated, all the names, characters, businesses, places, events and incidents in this book are either the product of the author's imagination or used in a fictitious manner. Any resemblance to actual persons, living or dead, or actual events is purely coincidental.

All rights reserved , Vishal Dixit, 2022, New Delhi, India.

CHAPTER ONE

INTRODUCTION

Year 2052 , There were many inventions in the world. Although space travel had become common at this time. But ,human desires were still not satisfied. Even at this time, scientists of many countries were involved in many types of researches.

By this time all the needs and amenities of man had been fulfilled. But where does it go, there is no end to the desire. Similarly, the inventions of the present time were completely based on the desire of man and the desire to get fame. The ongoing research at the present time was mainly carried out by the governments of many countries.

The researches conducted by the governments of the countries were mainly based on the defense system. In which new weapons were being discovered, perhaps the disastrous results of the atomic bomb were not able to satisfy man. And man wanted to invent more destructive weapons and he had succeeded to a great extent. By this time the bullets in the gun had been replaced by lasers which were originally based on the ignition system. But most of the bullets were still used because it was more lethal and cheaper.

The most frightening thing was that the goal of these researches was not the interest of the society, but the personal desire. Apart from the countries, many influential people who were very wealthy were also engaged in research to fulfill their desires, they had bought scientists by money to fulfill their craving, some of these influential people were such people who were wanted to disprove the biggest rules or say that indelible truth.

These people were spending most of their wealth for the fulfillment of their inferior desires and as it is the nature of the scientist, they also did not want to let that person's wealth go to waste. But the scientists had also taken the longing of the people as their goal, they were also making full use of their abilities, this time was completely based on scientific research and many good and bad results were happening in the world.

As far as the population is concerned, the global population had reached 9 billion and due to global laws, it was necessary to give citizenship to the citizens of other countries in the countries which had more area but less population so that the population density in a particular part. Do not exceed.

International organizations made this law after a special event, it was such that in the year 2041, the population of some countries had increased significantly. The population of only five major countries had reached 4.50 billion, due to which the population density increased and there was a situation of intolerance in hunger, recession, unemployment, the governments of these countries were not able to supply jobs and food for such a large population and for this reason. This created a feeling of resentment among the people towards the government.

At the beginning of 2042, in these 5 countries, about 200 million people died due to starvation and these deaths had a very negative effect on the mental level of the rest of the

people, a result of this was that people lost their temper
. There were religious and racial riots in these countries,
which the government of these countries was unable to
stop and the government of these countries sought help
from international organizations, so far 30 million people
had died in these religious and racial riots, which was the
biggest violence in history. But international organizations
brought the situation under control by sending a large
amount of army and relief material, but it was not easy for
them either.

After this incident, a group meeting was held by the
representatives of all the countries in which psychologists
and historians were also included and after the meeting
it was concluded that the root cause of this unpleasant
incident was increasing population density.

To solve this, this law was passed that the people of
these countries would be relocated to different countries.
Some intellectual psychologists suggested that to reduce the
possibility of such violence in future, the transfer should
be done on religious or racial scales rather than on other
Native citizens of countries can also behave violently with
relocated people.

Most of the countries agreed to this law but some of
the rich countries did not because according to them it was
an additional burden on them. These countries expressed
their consent against the law and wanted to use their
special powers, but due to 230 million deaths in just three
to four months, other countries forcefully persuaded the
wealthy countries.

Completely it took 14 months for population relocation,
but due to a great result, global peace was once again
established, although people did not forget that horrific
incident.

CHAPTER TWO

BEGINNING OF SINISTER INVENTIONS

At present, in 2052, there was an arms race between all the countries, maximum resources of nature were being used only in making weapons, but the weapons being made by the countries were only for defense.

The greatest danger to the world was from some people who were spending their money in research for their personal purpose because their intentions were not in the interest of world's good.

Although there were some public-friendly inventions, by this time all the work of man was being done by machines, due to which employment opportunities were limited, maximum employment was available in the service sector and people had to face a lot of difficulty in making a living.

Due to scientific research, a new employment had emerged, which was not very comfortable but was a good source of livelihood because scientific research was being done all over the world and some of these researches were also related to the medical field, in which new medicines were discovered. And also some defensive material which was used in the army. Human body was needed to test these inventions, due to which this need emerged as an employment, this employment was called **"Soldier of Science"**.

Because large-scale research was being done all over the world, this need was also very high. Due to which this employment was attracting a lot of poor people. However, it also had full security arrangements. If ever a drug had a bad effect on a person, then the treatment was already available for it. But still the mortality rate in this work area was 2 percent. And after death, compensation was given to the family of the person in the form of salary for the rest of his life and its details were given in advance.

In defense research, research was being done to increase the physical capacity of human beings, in which efforts were being made to increase the physical capacity of a normal human or say that strategic capability by many types of drugs, so that the army of that country could easily defeat other countries , although this thinking was of every country except a few.

In some countries, in order to increase the physical capacity of human beings, attempts were being made to match the DNA of other organisms by putting different characteristics of other organisms in the human body. And in these researches, the death rate of "soldiers of science" was the highest 35 percent, due to which their salary was highest in this particular type of research, but till now the success rate in this research was zero.

On the contrary, efforts were also being made by some countries to use other organisms in war, for which many types of scientific tests were done on those organisms and they were trained, they had also succeeded to a great extent in this effort, but This only came out as a negative result because even though those animals are physically more strong but mentally they could not compete with humans, due to which the years of hard work of these countries failed and they also faced defeat in war.

Because the displacement of population was done on racial and religious basis, due to this a new problem was exposed which was not anticipated by the global government. And each country wanted to prove its dominance over other countries, due to which the atmosphere of unrest in the world had once again arisen.

This global unrest had worried the governments and to deal with this situation, an international meeting was organized and the heads of all the countries were asked to find a solution to the problem through dialogue but this was not the only problem during the meeting. New news came out that there was a sudden 10 percent drop in the population of a monarchical country but the reasons behind it were still unknown.

All the countries had understood that some very dangerous research was being done by that monarchical country, but they could not find out the purpose behind these researches. To find out this, many countries had employed their intelligence departments.

It was revealed from some facts that the reason behind all these deaths was DNA modification and after so many deaths that country had got only two successes. But due to excessive loss of life and property, he now decided to stop this experiment. But it was a revolutionary beginning. This was the first breakthrough in research in this area, but its cost also could not be ignored. However, that country had flatly refused to expose its 2 successful tests to the world.

In view of the increasing conflict between countries, the global government had engaged its most skilled scientists to research a protective invention because the current situation could only be handled by science. After a few years, the best invention of the decade was made by scientists which could revolutionize the defense world and this invention was **"Dark Savior"**.

The **"Dark Savior"** was a light-blocking ray that blocked the particles of light falling in its path. Due to which there was a great darkness over that place, and by this the sunlight could be darkened.

It was used to avoid air attacks. "Dark Savior" used to make the places disappear by darkening and by this the path of the aircraft could also be darkened and it could be dropped and this weapon could also make the armies unable to see , due to which all the countries put an end to the conflict. Given because they did not have the device to deal with it and the global government kept this weapon in their hands. Gradually it was launched on every conflict frontier in space, due to which the struggle for domination in the world came to an end.

Even though peace had once again been established in the world, but the biggest danger was yet to come, which even the global government was unaware of.

CHAPTER THREE

EFFECTS ON NATURE

Due to the increasing population, due to the increasing construction work, the number of forests and plains was greatly reduced. Due to the decreasing number of forests and plains, the following animals have become extinct by this time.

i. Elephants v. Arctic fox
ii. Lions
iii. Rhinos
iv. Snow leopard

Due to increasing water pollution, even the following species of marine life had become extinct.

i. Alligators iv. Blue whales
ii. Hippos v. Ocean turtles
iii. Dolphins

There are also the following species of birds. By this time it had disappeared.

i. Vultures
ii. Swans

iii. Sparrows

iv. Hummingbirds

The process of extinction was not limited to birds only, but many types of insects and tree plant species had become extinct by this time.

Most of the rivers and ponds had dried up. Due to deforestation which reduced the annual rainfall. Alligators and hippopotamuses had become extinct due to the drying up of rivers and ponds.

However, hunting was the main reason for the disappearance of lions and snow leopards, which were being used for DNA modification.

70 percent of the world's glaciers had melted. Due to which most of the coastal areas were submerged, but in the present scientific era it was not a matter of much problem. Presently man had made habitats up to 71 meters below the water.

But taking lessons from all these things, trees and greenery were being given a lot of importance to the places of residence and there was a provision of even death penalty for destroying certain types of trees and plants because in present times nature is more important than the person. Was given to.

CHAPTER FOUR

INITIATIVE OF DESTRUCTION

As mentioned in the beginning of the book, some wealthy people were also involved in the race for these scientific researches, who were spending their money on these researches that too only for the fulfillment of their personal desires.

One of them was a person. "Doctor A" It had citizenships of many countries and this person did not believe in God and he himself was also a famous scientist and very rich person. He wanted to conquer the biggest truth of nature 'death', for which he was engaged in research work for almost 12 years.

Despite adopting various methods, till now its efforts were not successful . In the end, he decided that it is currently impossible to keep the human body alive forever, so why not try to preserve the most essential part of man, 'the brain'.

To discuss this decision, Dr. A invited a meeting with other scientists in which there were 8 very popular scientists from different countries and they all had one thing in common that they were all very greedy people for whom money was everything. . That is why all these scientists were supporting Dr. A in this selfish research.

At the time of meeting :

Dr. A : Today I have called all of you here to determine the direction of our research. As you all know, 12 years have passed since our mission **"The Infinite"** whose aim is to conquer death, but success is still not in our hands.

That's why I have decided that we should shift our attitude from the body to the brain because in the body all the parts of the body except the brain can be changed, which proves that the brain is the most essential part of the body. I want your views on how we can reach our objective by keeping the brain at the center.

All scientists get into thinking for a while.

Dr. Jason: Why don't we transplant one person's brain into another person's?

Dr. Tobey: This is not possible in present, to date no brain transplant has been successful.

Dr. Hannah: And the size of the brain of every person is different.

Dr. A: A person's whole life is organized in his brain, we have to think of some way by which memory of brain can be preserved and revived.

Dr. Shirish: We have to invent a machine by which the entire memory of the human brain can be saved in the computer and can be put in another body when needed.

Dr. Kiyasaki: And we will also need another machine to delete the current memory of the person's brain.

Dr. Xiang: With Doctor A, this task will not be too difficult.

Dr. Rutherford : We should start research work as soon as possible.

Dr. Kuzma: It will take about 3 years to make both these machines.

Dr. A: So then our new target will be to invent both the machines which we will have to complete in two and a half years. That's the end of this meeting.

This research work was being done secretly from the world government because its goal was not only for the society but only for the fulfillment of the desire of Doctor A.

A year and a half had passed since the research began, but only the invention of the brain's memory deletion machine was completed, which was named **"Brain Cleaner"**.

However, success was not yet achieved in the construction of the second machine. All the scientists were engaged in research day and night. Meanwhile some scientists were talking among themselves.

Dr. Kiyasaki: Let's take lunch break Dr. Shirish, you have been awake since last night.

Dr. Shirish: Doctor Kiyasaki You already know that I had suggested this machine, so the responsibility is more on me and now only 1 year is left.

Dr. Hannah: Yes, you are right and Dr. Kiyasaki has even completed the work of his invention.

Dr. Kiyasaki: No, I couldn't do this alone. It is only with the help of all of you that the invention has been completed so quickly.

Dr. Xiang: And now all of us together have to help in the invention of Dr. Shirish so that this research can be completed in time.

Dr. Jason: The research should be completed soon so that we can all go back to our families.

Dr. Rutherford: Yes, you are right, the last time we all went home one and a half years ago before this research started.

Dr. Hannah: Remembered from the family that Dr. Kiyasaki was married in that last 3 months' holiday.

Dr. Kiyasaki: (Shyly) Last year my wife's call came. My wife had given birth to a baby girl by now she must have been one year old, I was so busy with research that I haven't even seen her face yet.

Dr. Kuzma: Dr. Kiyasaki, You turned out to be very hidden, you didn't even tell us this.

Dr. Kiyasaki: Now this research should be completed as soon as possible so that I can meet my daughter.

Dr. Hannah: Let's celebrate the joy for Dr. Kiyasaki on becoming a father , belatedly today.

Dr. Xiang: And of course, let's invite Dr. A as well. Because of him, we do not have to worry about our family here and we are able to devote our full attention to research.

Dr. Shirish: Dr. A takes care of all the needs of our family. He keeps sending them money and all help from time to time.

While talking about this, all the scientists started dancing with joy and started preparing for the celebration. Although Dr. A could not attend this celebration, but he congratulated Dr. Kiyasaki and assured all the doctors of leave as soon as the research was completed. Along with this, a hefty amount was also promised as a reward.

After celebrating the whole day, all the scientists went to their respective rooms to rest and the next morning they again engaged in research.

Any scientist engaged in the research of **"The Infinite"** mission was prohibited from contact with his family or any outsider. Except on very important occasions, such as the death of a family member or the birth of a child, scientists were also prohibited from giving information about research to their relatives or anyone else.

Only 2 months were left in the time given by Dr. A and the construction of the machine was almost completed. Dr. Shirish and Dr. Xiang were engaged in preparations for its test and the rest of the scientists were engaged in solving the problems encountered in the test of 'Brain cleaner'.

In 'Brain Cleaner' all the memory of an organism's brain was deleted. Due to which the brain could not transmit signals to the body parts. Due to which after a few hours all the parts of the body stopped working and that organism died.

For this reason, before the invention of Dr. Shirish's machine, the human test of 'Brain cleaner' was stopped by Dr. A.

Because only the entire memory of the brain could be deleted by 'Brain cleaner'. This was the only problem before the scientists for which they had no solution.

On the other hand the preparations for the test had been completed and Dr. Shirish and Dr. Xiang were discussing on whom to conduct the test.

Dr. Shirish: Doctor Jiang Tell me, on which animal do you think this invention should be tested first?

Dr. Xiang: I think conventionally the first test should be done on rats.

Dr. Shirish: Why don't we try it on a dead mouse. If this machine can collect memory from the brains of dead rats, then we may be able to bring dead people to life.

Dr. Xiang: Great suggestion, let's start testing.

- The test was unsuccessful even after trying many times.

Dr. Xiang: This try was a failure, let's test on alive rats.

Even after testing on about a dozen rats, it was not successful and all the rats died.

In this, doctor Hannah comes over there, (hesitatingly) Dr. Shirish how did so many rats die, why is this machine not working on them?

Dr. Shirish: By looking at it, it seems that because the brain of these mice is very small. Due to which their brain is not able to bear the weight of the machine, so all these rats have died of brain failure.

Dr. Hannah: That means we would have to test it on a large brain's animal.

Dr. Shirish: Not only the big size but that animal should have more intellectual capacity.

Dr. Xiang: Then tell us, on which animal will our next test be?

Dr. Shirish: Now we would have to test it on monkeys, and again we have to start with a dead monkey.

Dr. Xiang: (Surprisingly) That means the hope of reviving dead is still on.

Dr. Shirish: Yes!

Almost every type of dead and living organisms were collected in the laboratory's storehouse so that scientists could experiment on them when the time came.

Dr. Shirish and Dr. Xiang brought 2 dead and 2 alive monkeys for testing.

In the storehouse, the dead animals were kept in large glass boxes and in a cool place to prevent them from rotting. The sight of the storehouse was so frightening that a common man could faint just by looking at it.

By this time all the scientists had come here.

Dr. Jason: So now you are preparing to test on monkeys.

Dr. Xiang: Yes doctor, because the test on rats was unsuccessful .

Dr. Tobey: Dr. Xiang, why don't you direct test it on humans. We didn't invent this machine to revive monkeys.

All scientists starts laughing mercilessly.

Dr. Shirish: Doctor Tobey You already know how expensive it is to conduct tests on humans and if the 'Soldier of Science' dies during the test, then we have to bear the cost of his family for the rest of their life.

Dr. Hannah: And this also affects the research budget and Dr. A has promised us that the remaining money of this research budget will be distributed among all of us, so why should we do our loss?

Dr. Rutherford: Dr. Hannah you are pure evil.

All the scientists burst our laughing. Even at this time, scientists were more concerned about budget money than human life.

Dr. Kiyasaki: And anyway, test on humans can only be done in the presence of Dr. A.

Dr. Kuzma: Ever since the formation of this **SSO**, it has become extremely difficult to test on humans.

(SSO: SOLDIERS OF SCIENCE ORGANISATION)

Dr. Tobey: Yes, it is because of this organization that this class (soldier of science) has got so much protection and rights.

Dr. Jason: That company of Doctor A is being run in the name of Medical Research Company. That's why we get 'Soldiers of science' easily for testing.

Dr. Tobey: Don't give them so much respect by calling them 'soldiers of science'. They are those people of the society who could not develop along with the world. To us they are no more than the pigs kept in the laboratory.

All the scientists agreed with Dr. Tobey and started laughing.

Dr. Shirish: First test will be done on dead monkeys.

Even after trying many times, Dr. Shirish could not collect memory from the dead monkey's brain.

Dr. Jason: Dr. Shirish, let's test on alive monkeys.

Many attempts at this time also failed, due to which the monkey's heart rate fell again and again.

Dr. Hannah: Dr. Shirish, give this monkey an adrenaline shot and try again.

Dr. Shirish: It's a great advice.

The trial was started by giving the monkey an adrenaline shot, this time the test was successful and the machine successfully collected the entire memory from the monkey's brain, although the monkey went into unconsciousness.

Machine had completed it's first work (collection of memory from brain).

All the scientists were extremely thrilled with the receipt of the first stage of the machine.

After a few minutes that monkey died because all the memory had been removed from the monkey's brain. Due to which gradually the body parts of the monkey stopped working.

However, the scientists were so happy about their success that they did not pay attention to it. According to him the monkey was just unconscious.

Dr. Xiang: Congratulations Dr. Shirish, what would you name your this new invention.

Dr. Shirish: This is not my only invention but of all of us, and it is a matter of its name, it would be more appropriate to name this machine when it completes its work, that is, when its second phase is also completed.

Dr. Kiyasaki: Dr. Shirish, let's try to put this memory in the brain of another dead monkey.

Dr. Rutherford: Yes, if this would be possible, then even if not the dead person , but the dead body can definitely be revived.

All scientists agreed and started testing. Despite several attempts, no signal could come from the dead monkey's brain and it was unsuccessful.

Dr. Shirish:

Dr. Shirish: To transfer the memory to the brain, electricity present in the brain is required, which is not present in the brain of a dead organism. That's why the test failed.

Memory transfer by machine was successful but monkey died by heart stroke. Scientists concluded that because of extra pressure over brain the monkey died.

After this all the scientists decided that the brain in which the memory is to be inserted. It will be first deleted with ' Brain cleaner'. But after deleting the memory with 'Brain cleaner', the creature used to die within an hour. For this reason, the work of memory transfer will have to be completed within 1 hour from Dr. Shirish's machine.

All scientists did the same and this test was successful, However, in this process only one could be kept alive. With 40 days remaining, the scientists had completed the mission **"The Infinite"** and its information was given to Doctor A for testing on humans.

Dr. Shirish named his machine **"The Divine Touch"** .

The research revealed the following facts which were sent to the Dr. A.

- **The Divine Touch** could neither retrieve memory from the dead brain nor could it be revived by inserting memory into the dead brain.
- Memory could only be inserted into an empty brain by **The Divine Touch.** Due to which its use was not possible without 'Brain cleaner'.

- It was not even possible to re-insert the brain from which the memory was extracted by **The Divine Touch**, because in this process the organism would die within a few minutes.
- **The Divine Touch** could save a person's memory in a computer.
- Its use by scientists was suggested by **The Divine Touch** that a person could be transferred to another body with all his memory so that he could live for eternity.

Another fact came to the fore in the research, due to which it became very necessary to use brain cleaner in this process.

When the memory of another brain was inserted in the monkey's brain, along with the memory, the **'Autonomic nervous system'** located in the brain was also transferred, this was the part of the brain that runs the respiratory system, heart rate, blood pressure, digestive system of the body. Due to the arrival of dual 'Autonomic nervous system' in the brain, the heart rate, respiration, blood pressure doubled, due to which the monkey died of intoxication, heart attack and brain failure.

Therefore, before transferring the memory, it became very important to delete the current memory and for this reason the role of 'Brain cleaner' also became very important.

The Divine Touch couldn't be used for the memory cleaner because after this process the creature would die within a few minutes. And in these few minutes it was impossible to transfer the memory. On the other hand after the use of 'Brain cleaner' The creature could be kept alive for 80 minutes by ventilator.

After reading that report Dr. A congratulated the scientists for the completion of mission and said them to rest and also fixed the date for human testing. Till that all scientists were sent to Dr. A's special island for rest but even there they didn't had the permission to contact with the outer world or people.

While resting on the island all scientists were talking with each other.

Dr. Kiyasaki: Dr. Shirish what do you thinks? We have made that revolutionary invention. How much fame will we get when it comes in front of the world?

Dr. Shirish: You are right, The names of eight of us will be written in the pages of history.

Dr. Xiang: With our this invention, we would be able to give immortality to the world's rich people, scientists, politicians and artists.

Dr. Tobey: And in return, we will be able to charge a hefty amount from them.

Dr. Hannah: I am waiting for our money so that I can spend the rest of my life comfortably.

Dr. Rutherford: If we make many machines like that, then world's every person can become immortal.

Dr. Kiyasaki: I just wants to finish human testing as soon as possible to meet my daughter.

The test date had arrived. All the scientists and Dr. A had come to the laboratory.

Because this machine's goal was to transfer the memory from brain, For that Dr. A had intentionally called a 54 years old and a 22 years young 'Soldier of science' for testing.

Dr. A: (Addressing the scientists) All of you meet them, He is Mr. Lawrence(22) and Mr. Brown(54). These both 'Soldiers of science' will help us today in our testing.

Mr. Lawrence and Mr. Brown shakes hands with all scientists and greets them.

Mr. Lawrence was involved in an experiment for the first time. While Mr. Brown had been in the business for 35 years, Mr. Brown, seeing Mr. Lawrence frightened, goes to talk to him as all the scientists are preparing for the test.

Mr. Brown: Mr. Lawrence are you involved in an experiment for the first time?

Mr. Lawrence: You can call me Lawrence, Yes I'm appearing in an experiment for the first time.

Mr. Brown : Son, are you frightened?

Mr. Lawrence: To be honest, Yes.

Mr. Brown: There is nothing to be frightened son, look at me I am in this business from 35 years and totally healthy. All the security arrangements have already been made by the scientists. So don't worry unnecessarily.

Mr. Lawrence: Thank you for giving me courage.

Mr. Brown: How many members are in your family?

Mr. Lawrence: Me, my mother and a younger sister(13) ,my father died in the 1942 riots. And in your family?

Mr. Brown: Me, my wife(51) and a son(23).

Mr. Lawrence: Why your son lets you do this work?

Mr. Brown: My son is mentally weak since childhood. He does not even know how to speak father properly. (Tears come to Mr. Brown's eyes by saying this).

Mr. Lawrence: I am sorry.

Mr. Brown: No problem son, now I would not be able to do this work for long. Because now there is very little time left. I just wish I could die in some trial. So that my family can spend the rest of their life from the insurance money.

Mr. Lawrence: Don't say that, everything would be fine.

In between that all scientists were talking together.

Dr. Kiyasaki: All preparations are almost done.

Dr. Xiang: As all of you knows, that only one of those 'soldiers of science' could stay alive in this experiment. So, shall we tell this thing to them.

Dr. Tobey: Don't be a fool, they should be proud that their life would be a use of this great invention. You don't have to be worried about them, after all their lives are still hell.

Dr. Hannah:

Dr. Hannah: And it may also happen that when they come to know about this, they refuse to in experiment. Then it will be difficult to arrange for another person so soon and our life of luxury will be delayed further.

All scientists agreed and laughed. Dr. A decided that Mr. Brown's memory will be transferred into Mr. Lawrence's brain. Because the purpose of this invention was to provide a new and healthy body to a person near death.

- Mr. Brown's reports clarified that his death was near , For this reason he was not included in current researches. But for Dr. A's experiment, Mr. Brown was best.

Dr. Hannah: How wasteful it would be that such a young boy would die, yet the body would still be alive.

The trial had begun , Mr. Lawrence and Mr. Brown had been sedated.

Dr. Kiyasaki: Let's delete Lawrence's brain memory with the help of 'Brain cleaner'.

After deleting Lawrence's memory, Mr. Brown's memory extracted in the computer with the help of **"The Divine Touch"**. Almost in 40 minutes Mr. Brown's memory transferred into Mr. Lawrence's brain.

Mr. Shirish: All the testing work has been done. Now just waiting for Mr. Brown to come to his senses.

After some time when Mr. Brown came to his senses, then he was shocked to find himself in Lawrence's body. And all scientists started congratulating each other on the success of experiment. However, nothing was told about Lawrence to Mr. Brown.

Dr. A: (Addressing everyone) Now all of you go to your respective rooms and relax. It's been a long night. Tomorrow a party will be held for the success of our mission. So you all take a good rest tonight.

All scientists and Mr. Brown went to their respective rooms.

Around 1:45 PM, Doctor Hannah was found walking into Mr. Brown's (now in Lawrence's body) room, and at 4:00 PM she went back to her room. Yet all this was not saved from the intelligence cameras installed by Dr. A. Doctor A had installed intelligence cameras in the entire laboratory and all the scientists' rooms so that they could be monitored and this was not known to anyone except Doctor A. Although Doctor A used to ignore such situations.

Next day all the scientists and Mr. Brown reach the party and after having fun all day, after having dinner in the evening, they come back and sleep in their respective rooms. The next morning all the scientists' rooms were ringing with alarms but no one was going to turn them off because all the scientists and Mr. Brown were dead.

Because Dr. A wanted to keep his invention hidden from the world, and by that he wanted to achieve immortality, that's why he had all the scientists and Mr. Brown killed by putting poison in the party's food.

A message has been sent to the families of all the scientists that all the scientists are engaged in new research. And a message was sent to the families of Mr. Lawrence and Mr. Brown that our experiment was unsuccessful and they died, and they were being compensated every month.

But mere compensation could not reduce their suffering. Mister Lawrence's mother died a few months later in grief over the death of her son, and Lawrence's sister was left alone. On the other hand Mr. Brown's wife took care of herself and decided to get her son treated with the compensation money.

CHAPTER FIVE

END

Because all the countries around the world had turned on religious and racial groups. But democracy still prevailed. However, politicians were given the title of ruler and the election of the new head leader was also in the hands of only a few bigwigs. The vote of the people was negligible.

Doctor A's medical research company was world famous. That is why, he always had the big people of the world, the rulers and politicians of the countries always coming to him. And it was also a big source of income for Doctor A. The most powerful country at this time had monarchy. And one day the king of there Mr. White came to Doctor A with his retarded son.

Mr. Hopkin: Dr. A king white has arrived, and he is waiting for you in the guest room. (Mr. Hopkin was Doctor A's oldest trusted companion and he had also welcomed King White).

Dr. A: I'm coming.

Doctor A reaches the room and welcomes King White with a handshake and expresses his gratitude on his arrival.

King White: Doctor A, today I have come to you with a very special work. You all know that ever since you cured my old cold, we have considered you as our family doctor.

Dr. A: (Admittedly) It is a matter of pride for me. Doctor A knew that any good doctor could cure that cold, but because of having too much money, King White chose Doctor A.

King White used to visit Doctor A even for minor ailments, which caused frequent interruptions in Doctor A's research. Therefore, Doctor A disliked King White. Although King White was the ruler of the most powerful country in the world, it was not in the hands of Doctor A to refuse him.

But reaching out to a famous scientist like Dr. A on small matters was like 'killing a bird with a cannon'.

Dr. A: Tell me King White, how can I help you?

King White gestured and asked his companions and Mr. Hopkin to leave the room. He wanted to talk to the doctor in solitude.

King White: Doctor A You already know that next year I have to declare one of my sons as king and my eldest son is retarded since childhood and other two sons are against me. If I make any of them king, it is possible that they will get me hanged as soon as they become king.

Dr. A: Then why don't you throw your those sons out of country?

King White: If I do that, then who will become the next king. Then maybe the world government will take over my kingdom.

Dr. A: What do you wants from me?

King White : Dr. A, I wants you to cure my eldest son, If he becomes well then I will make him the next king and I will hang my two sons which are against me. I knows that this work would not be hard for you.

Doctor A was pleased to hear this and immediately agreed to that work and asked King White for 2 weeks. A huge conspiracy had taken birth in the mind of Doctor A. King White returns to his kingdom after leaving his son (Nicholas White).

Mr. Hopkin: Doctor A Why didn't you tell King White about our mission "The Infinite"?

Dr. A: No Hopkin, If I had told him about our mission, So he would have forcibly snatched our invention from us and would have ruled this racially divided world forever. Our invention can change this world Hopkin. And now the time has come that now the rule of these foolish intellects will end and we will become the new ruler of this whole world and not just the ruler. 'We will become the new Gods of this world'. (Saying this, Doctor A starts laughing out loud).

Dr. A was an atheist, and he wanted to finish all religions of the world. His ideology was that 'a human can do anything with the power of his brain'.

Mr.Hopkin: Dr. A, I didn't understand what are you trying to say.

Dr. A: Hopkin, we are not going to cure Nicholas White.

Mr. Hopkin: But Dr. A, you have promised King White.

Dr. A: You already knows Hopkin, that my body has become old now, and it would not be able stay alive for long. And even though Nicholas White is a retard. Still, being from the royal family, his body is very strong. And all parts are in best condition. So we should not let this opportunity pass our hands.

Mr. Hopkin: Dr. A, what do you thinks, will you be able to cheat King White?

Dr. A: Hopkin, I wants you to use our invention and transfer my brain into Nicholas White's brain. Take care of my body. Unless I instruct you again and keep in mind that this matter should remain between the two of us.

Hopkin did the same and after some time Dr. A was inside Nicholas White's body. Doctor A was overjoyed to feel young again.

Dr. A: (Arrogantly) Hopkin, 'I am the new upcoming God of this world'.

Dr. A made a false report of Nicholas White, that operation was successful but Nicholas doesn't have his old memories, although he had become very intelligent and can learn and understand anything easily. This report was made and sent to King White.

King White felt a little sad after reading the report, but he was more than happy because now he could make his eldest son king. King White sent a message that he was coming to pick up his son tomorrow.

Next day King White comes at the laboratory and Mr. Hopkin welcomes him.

King White: Mr. Hopkin, call Dr. A, where is he, I am grateful to him and I wants to thank him.

Mr. Hopkin: Sorry! But Dr. A has gone for his other research. He is not here.

King White: This is bad. How would I thank him now. Still I will give you the double amount of fixed as a token of gratitude.

Mr. Hopkin: Let's meet prince Nicholas.

King White: (After reaching in Nicholas's room) Nicholas, son what are you doing?

Nicholas White: Father, you have came, happy to see you, I was just reading a novel.

King White was overjoyed to see his son speak and read well. And tears of joy came from his eyes and he embraced Nicholas. Although King White was unaware of this thing, that Dr. A was inside Nicholas's body. King White thanked Hopkin again and returned to his country taking Prince

Nicholas with him.

After some time news comes that Doctor A has died suddenly due to cardiac arrest. However it was only a ploy by Doctor A (who was now in Nicholas White's body) to destroy his body in the eyes of society. And the instructions to spread this news have already been given by Dr. A. to Mr. Hopkin.

The news of Dr. A's death was shocking for whole world, because he was world's most popular scientist. And world's bigwigs became very sad after knowing that because they used to visit Dr. A time to time. At the death ceremony of Dr. A. the world's big people came to pay their last farewell to him, including King White and Prince Nicholas.

(Note: Because now Dr. A was inside Nicholas White's body, so for better understanding we will now call him Nicholas A.)

King White: (Addressing condolence meet) Dr. A was like my close friend, I am sad that I could not even thank him while he was alive.

Nicholas A: Dr. A was a very nice person. He took care of me as like a father and cured me. I am very grateful to him.(Saying that Nicholas A starts to shed false tears).

Every person in the condolence meet was very sad, but one person was most unhappy after hearing the news of Dr. A, and she was Miss Venus(14) , Miss Venus knew about the reality of Dr. A and she hated Dr. A very much. And Miss Venus wanted to gather some information from Dr. A, which became impossible now with the news of Dr. A's death. After burying Dr. A's body everybody returned.

After returning to his kingdom, King White was worried about his younger sons. He was thinking that his those two sons who were against him should be hanged or be thrown out of country. At this point, Nicholas A arrives in King

White's room.

Nicholas A: Father, why are you so tensed?

King White: Son, I am just thinking about your brothers, that they should be hanged or be thrown out of country?

Nicholas A: If we throws them out of country ,then it might be possible that they will tell our military secrets to the enemy countries, it could be dangerous for us. And even if hanged, many ministers and subjects can protest.

King White: Then what is your suggestion ?

Nicholas A: Why don't we send these two to Mr. Hopkin, these two could be a use in their experiments. And Dr. A's favor will also be a little less in your mind.

King White: And what would we say to their mother and ministers.

Nicholas A: Send me also with them ,and tell everyone that you have sent your three sons to see world famous Dr. A's various inventions and to learn something.

Nicholas White who was once a retard, after hearing that good solution from him King White shocked. And embraced him while praising his intellect. And did as he said. Even after that suggested there was a huge conspiracy of Nicholas A, which only he knew.

Even before King White's three sons arrive at Doctor A's laboratory, King White receives a message sent by Hopkin. According to that message because Doctor A had no heir. Therefore, Doctor A had declared all his property to be heir to Prince Nicholas. King White was very happy to read this message. Nicholas A and two princes reaches at Dr. A's laboratory, after reaching there Nicholas A directs Hopkin.

Nicholas A: Hopkin, I wants to transfer your memory into King White's youngest son's brain. So you could come with me and also help me there.

Hopkin deletes the memory of King White's two younger sons under the pretext of a general health test. And Nicholas A puts Hopkin's memory in the youngest son's brain.

After this, Doctor A and Hopkin together save their invention elsewhere and set the laboratory on fire and come back to King White and inform that the Middle Prince and Hopkin died due to the fire in the laboratory.

It was the time of Nicholas A to become the king, King White was surprised by his youngest son's changed behavior ,but this change was in his favor that's why he was happy.

After becoming the King, Nicholas A hanged King White , and announced in front of the world that he is not Nicholas A but 'Dr. A' . Who transferred his memory to the body of Nicholas White with the help of his invention **"The Divine Touch"** and also states that with the help of his invention **"The Divine Touch"** A person near death could be given a new life or say a body.

After this announcement of Dr. A, there is a bustle in the whole world. The global government also organizes meeting regarding this situation.

(Note: Because now Dr. A announced about his real identity, so addressing him Dr. A from now would be fine)

Mr. Garfield: (Head of Global Government) This fact is surprising that Dr. A is alive, but the matter which is of more concern is his invention, from which he is claiming to give new life to the person who is near to death.

Mr. Adam: (Senior Executive of Global Government) That dangerous invention should not be in the hands of a person, otherwise unrest will spread into the whole world , so we have to attain that invention in the hands of global government as soon as possible. Otherwise it's result would be very fearsome. "The World which shall be feared".

Miss Daisy: (Investigator of Global Government) But it would not be that easy to take that invention from Dr. A, because now he has become the King of most powerful country, if we tries to take that invention from him forcefully ,then there can be a lot of loss of life and property and even after that our victory is not certain.

Other people were also involved in this meeting but they just seems to be agreeing.

Mr. Garfield: In view of the current situation, now we can only keep an eye over Dr. A, but we can't do anything against him. With this decision meeting ended.

On the other hand Hopkin comes in Dr. A's room.

Dr. A: Hopkin, How did you come at this time?

Mr. Hopkin: Dr. A, why did you exposed about our invention and your identity, wouldn't it be dangerous for us?

Dr. A: Hopkin, Now I have become ruler of this country, with that a very large military power came to us, So now no one will be so foolish as to try to snatch our invention from us. To put it bluntly, we have become very powerful. And only by telling about this invention we can take advantage of it and change this world according to us. You see, soon many people will be with us.

Mr. Hopkin: That means all these things are a part of your plan.

Dr. A: Yes Hopkin, It's been 1 year since our invention was completed. Now is the time to start our plan.

Miss Venus was most happy to hear the news of Doctor A being alive because her hope was rekindled.

Miss Venus: Finally, I would be able to know the reason behind my brother's death.

Dr. A was cause of many people's death. So it was still a mystery about who Miss Venus was talking about. But one thing was sure that Miss Venus hated Dr. A very much.

As the news of **"The Divine Touch"** spread, so did the great people around the world contacted Doctor A because he wanted to conquer all death. At this time, Doctor A, seeing a large number of people, had demanded a huge amount in return, which only the people of the upper strata could pay. Doctor A doubled the economy of his country with the help of **"The Divine Touch"** within a year, which greatly increased his power. Also, all the people whom Doctor A gave new life with the help of his invention, they also got along with Doctor A.

Because of these experiments almost 5000 ' soldiers of science' died in a year. Because of which now the **SSO** flatly refused to supply 'Soldiers of science' to Dr. A.

This decision of the **SSO** had created a big problem in front of Dr. A. But now he was not the earlier Doctor A but the King Doctor A and he had found a solution to this problem as well. Doctor A recruited in the name of military posts in his country to fill the body in his experiments because most people wanted a new young body through **"The Divine Touch"**. Therefore, only young and healthy people were kept in these recruitments and only poor people applied in this. This was a very cruel decision, which signifies that Dr. A did not cared a bit about other people's lives. Global government was aware of it, but it was unable to do anything.

About 2 years later, Doctor A comes across a report from his country which included the results of **"The Divine Touch"**.

Positive results:-

- With the help of **"The Divine Touch"** the economy of Dr. A's country had become 40 percent of the world.
- Doctor A had acquaintance with the heads and powerful people of many countries.
- Because of being the biggest economy Dr. A's country had become more powerful.
- Also from many activists of the global government, Dr. A's good relations were established.

Negative results:-

- Due to the excess of these experiments, the existence of many poor people was disappearing and due to the involvement of young children in these experiments, the old parents became helpless.
- The cycle of death had stopped in the big and rich families. Due to which their population was increasing gradually, but at the same time their share in wealth was also increasing.
- Due to which the new generation started killing the elders in order to take possession of the property because the dead person could not be brought to life by **"The Divine Touch"**.

Murders could also have been avoided by the use of **"The Divine Touch"**. The way only Doctor A knew, which he had kept hidden from the world until now because that was the real power of **"The Divine Touch"**.

On the whole, only Dr. A was benefited from these results and only other people were directly or indirectly harmed but still everything was going according to the plan of Dr. A. Still Dr. A arranged a meeting to discuss these results in which many country heads took part.

Dr. A: All of you must have read this report, if we do not take some decision regarding this now, then the future situation will become very frightening.

Mr. Brian: If the conditions remain like this, then gradually the population of poor people will be very less and the population of rich people will increase.

Miss Valentine: And yet the population growth will be higher than the death rate because the birth rate is the same in both the groups.

Mr. Max: At this rate, the population will continue to grow, due to which there will be a shortage of resources in the future.

Mr. Page: So, in present we have to think of a way of population control.

Dr. A: And you all have to apply this new rule in your countries too. Because situations are also same there.

Mr. Max: But about which rule you are talking about ?

Dr. A: To stop the increasing population we have to stop birth rate first, So now we will prohibit poor people from having children and only certain people will be allowed to have children. Rich people and people whose children can be used for future use in **"The Divine Touch"**. It would be the new 'Population Act' of our world.

Mr. Brian: This would be a very cruel law.

Miss Valentine: Dr. A, our country is not monarchist like yours. And we are also. And we also have to answer global government, if global government doesn't interferes ,only then it is possible.

Mr. Page: Dr. A, in present your country is strongest. So why don't you attack on global government and take them under your control.

Dr. A: It is true that global government can not compete us in military power, but there is only one reason. Because of that our victory is still not certain.

Mr. Max: And what is it? Dr. A.

Dr. A: (Gravely) It is 'Dark Savior'. It is the greatest power of global government, otherwise I would have attacked them by now. Let us first implement this law in our country. (With this result the meeting ends).

After some time this law is implemented. And his children were forcibly taken away from the violators of this law. There is a situation of intolerance in the whole country. The life of the poor section, which was already very difficult, now becomes more pathetic.

By **"The Divine Touch"** not only old people were given new life, but also deceased children , Disabled, and young people were given new bodies. For that there was a need of every age group bodies. And by implementing this law Dr. A had arranged for this need as well.

On the other hand, Mr. Garfield, the head of the global government, suffers from severe health problems and is diagnosed with a very serious illness, which he cannot get treatment due to the cost of its treatment. In such a situation, his family members ask to take the help of Doctor A. But for the use of **"The Divine Touch"**, doctors charged huge sums of money, which was impossible for Mr. Garfield to meet.

Mr. Garfield was always against Dr. A's this invention and policies, but because of the fear of death he goes to meet Dr. A to get his help. This was a golden opportunity for Dr. A.

While meeting:-

Dr. A: Mr. Garfield, as I told the charge for this operation would be a hundred million.

Mr. Garfield: Dr. A, I can not afford that huge amount , can you help me?

Dr. A: Mr. Garfield, I can do this operation for you absolutely free, but on one condition, that your global government will have to come in my support.

Fearing death, Mr. Garfield agrees to all of Doctor A's conditions, and the global government comes out in support of Doctor A. As soon as the global government comes in support of Doctor A, all the friendly countries of Doctor A implement Population Act in their respective countries so that the life of the people of the lower strata becomes very miserable. Because now Doctor A was being supported by the global government, so now Doctor A had also taken the **"Dark savior"** in his hands and his country was already very powerful and the countries who refused to support Doctor A. Those countries were forcibly occupied by invading by Doctor A. And merged into his own country.

With the implementation of the 'Population Act', there was a ban on the birth of children of the poor and weaker sections and some weaker sections were allowed to have children. That too only so that they can be used in the future in "The Divine Touch". Living in such a pathetic condition, the people of the lower strata gradually lose faith in God and religion and because the rich people did not fear death. That's why they start thinking of themselves as God. The people of both sections gradually stopped going to religious places. And with time, the followers of all religions and sects decrease. Dr. A was very pleased with this result because he was always a true atheist and wanted to destroy all religions.

The world was still divided into many countries. Although everyone was a supporter of Dr. A, this was not liked by the Dr. A. So he sent a proposal to merge all the countries into Dr. A's country. But all the countries disagreed on this point and 23 countries started the war by forming a faction against Doctor A.

However this attempt was unsuccessful, With great military power and the help of the **Dark Savior**, Dr. A defeated the opposing faction and takes over all the countries. In this way, at present, Dr. A had merged all the countries of the world into his country. In this way the **Dark Savior**, once considered the savior of the world, became the cause of the destruction of the world.

Because now Dr. A had become the ruler of the whole world, so he did not needed money anymore. He handed over the responsibility of different provinces to his friends and supporters. However, he still continued to use "**The Divine Touch**" for his friends, supporters and loved ones. And the 'Population Act' also continued.

The inner humanity of individuals was destroyed by so many changes in the world. It became foolish to think about helping someone. Because all the religions were slowly disappearing and the present world needed a new religion so that they could continue on this path because it is clear that religion does not require the individual but the individual needs religion.

For completing this need, Dr. A started a new religion. And Dr. A and his millions of supporters adopted this new religion. The people who feared from Dr. A become his supporters. This new religion or shall we say cult was named **"The Trust"** . The followers of this religion believed that if a person trusts on him/herself then everything is possible, and his/her trust possesses the power of doing everything. In this religion mirrors were placed in the place of God's statues, So that the self-confidence of the person increases, and the feeling of being his own God will develop.

Dr. A's this cult was highly supported, And soon the number of supporters of **"The Trust"** religion reached billions. However some people still stick to their old religions because Doctor A never forced conversions. People had adopted the religion **"The Trust"** after losing hope and being influenced by his ideas.

In **Trust** religion practice of mirror worshipping became popular. Due to which the worshiper was filled with confidence psychologically by seeing his image in the mirror and this religion also became successful.

On the other Mr. Hopkin was talking with Dr. A.

Mr. Hopkin: Dr. A, what is the objective of this new religion.

Dr. A: Hopkin, the objective of our new religion is to make people self dependent.

Think what people used to do before. They used to tell their sorrows in front of the idols of the deities and expected some kind of miracle from the deities that the gods would save them from their sorrows. But in this religion, where a person is his own deity, when he tells his sorrows and troubles to the mirror, then by looking at his face in the mirror, he understands that only I can get myself out of all this and with confidence, he puts in efforts. And their belief in themselves is what makes them successful.

Religions never meant that a person should depend on miracles and forget his abilities, but some hypocrites made religion the den of miracles and took away his confidence and hard work from the person. That's why I had to start this religion. I was never against any religion, but depending on someone in the name of religion and forgetting our capabilities and responsibilities. I did not liked these things.

In present your watches, that some people are still connected to their old religions, **these are people which are not dependent on religion. But for them religion is only a way to thank our creator**, because of that these people did not blamed gods for present situation and are still adamant to their religions. These people don't needs our changes, but the whole world is going to become like them.

Hopkin shocked after hearing those words from Dr. A. With this a decade comes to an end and along with the decade, different religions, sects, countries and the inner humanity of man also comes to an end.

Dr. A used "**The Divine Touch**" not only for the wealthy and his loved ones, but also for those who had special talents. Whether he/she was poor or rich, because Dr. A wanted to create a world in which no one was useless. In clear words, he was trying to mold the world according to himself.

CHAPTER SIX

STRUGGLE

In this age, most of the works was done by machines. And the main source of income of little educated lower strata's people was to become 'Soldier of science'. But now this employment was also terminated by Dr. A. Because he had arranged it himself. And those who died in this business in the past, now their families have also stopped getting the amount of compensation. Because of which the life of these people had become very pathetic now, but people could not understand the reason behind it. Except for one person who was Miss Venus.

Miss Venus was 18 years old and she was a very intelligent girl. She lived alone. And, for so many years, the amount of compensation for his brother used to come. She used to spend it only for her studies, sustenance and gathering information about Doctor A. She had been collecting information related to Dr. A for so many years and she found out that Dr. A's research in which her brother had died. Another 'Soldier of Science' also died in the same research.

When she get to know that another 'Soldier of science' died in that research, So she decides to meet their family to gather more information. Miss Venus never believed that the only reason for her brother's death was the failure of an experiment. And upon learning that another 'Soldier of Science' had died in that research. The suspicion of Miss Venus intensifies.

Miss Venus: (Holding Mr. Lawrence's picture in her hand) Brother, I will definitely find out the truth behind your death. If your death will proved to be murder, then I will definitely take revenge on Doctor A.

Miss Venus visits Mr. Brown's family. Mr. Brown's home was middle-class.

Miss Venus: Are you Mrs. Brown?

Mrs. Brown: Yes I am. Who are you?

Miss Venus: I am Venus, younger sister of Mr. Lawrence. My 22 year old elder brother also died in the same research in which your husband died 5 years ago. I want to talk to you about the same.

Mrs. Brown: Sad to know, how can I help you?

Miss Venus: Can you tell me something about that research. In which Mr. Brown was involved.

Mrs. Brown: I don't knows much about that, but at that time a health report of Mr. Brown was arrived. According to that his death was close , because of that no one was including him in their researches from a long time, that's why our situations went very bad, but then even after knowing everything , Dr. A included Mr. Brown in his research.

Miss Venus: Shortly after his death, Doctor A told the world about **"The Divine Touch"**. Maybe Mr. Brown and my brother were involved in the research of **"The Divine Touch"**.

Mrs. Brown: What do you wants to say?

Miss Venus: Mrs. Brown I mean if my brother and Mr. Brown were involved in the research of **"The Divine Touch"** then the cause of their death could not be the failure of the test because it was a successful test. This is why "**The Divine Touch**" exists today. That means Mr. Brown and my brother were murdered by Dr. A.

Mrs. Brown: But, why would he do that, he is a good person. He always sent the compensation money on time. Because of which I was able to get my son treated.

Miss Venus: (Shockingly) he is a good person? Don't you see the condition of the poor people of the world? He killed them so that his invention could remain a secret until the time came.

So Mrs. Brown's son arrives who used to work in a private company. Mrs. Brown introduces Venus and his son.

Mrs. Brown: Venus, how many members are in your family?

Miss Venus: I lives alone, After my brother's death, my mother also died of shock.

Mrs. Brown: Sorry, tell us something about Lawrence.

Miss Venus: My brother was a very intelligent and optimistic person. He wanted to become a scientist, and wanted to invent such. With the help of which once again all the people in the world could live in harmony. But after my father's death in 2042's racial riots we had to relocate, and we were left with no means of livelihood. When looking for work for a long time, no work was found yet. So my brother decided to become a 'Soldier of Science'.

(With tears in her eyes) It was the first research of my brother in which he was included, he was frightened a lot, but for us he went there.

After saying this, Miss Venus starts crying. Mrs. Brown and Ian calm Venus down and say don't worry, we are with you. Ian Brown(27) was Mrs. Brown's son. Miss Venus leaves thanking Mrs. Brown and Ian, and promise to come next week.

Venus reaches home and finds out about Ian Brown, that which health institution treated Ian. Gathering information, she learnt that Ian was treated by Doctor A's company. Knowing this, Venus suspects that, instead of treating Ian Brown, like Nicholas White, Dr. A may have sent one of his detectives to replace Ian with the help of **"The Divine Touch"**. So that if anyone in future reaches Mrs. Brown to learn about that research, Doctor A would know.

With this thought, Venus becomes alert. And the next week, does not visit Mrs. Brown. And go to another city for a few days so that the people of Dr. A do not come to her house looking for Venus. A month later, when Venus returns, she learns from her neighbors that no one has come to her house for so many days. Then Miss Venus realizes that she was overthinking and decides to go back to Mrs. Brown's house.

Venus, reached at Mrs. Brown's house and talked with Mrs. Brown and Ian Brown.

Mrs. Brown: Venus, where were you from so long? You promised to come last month.

Miss Venus: Pardon me Mrs. Brown, I went to other city for an important work.

Mrs. Brown: (Watching cross in Venus's neck) Venus, why didn't you adopted **The Trust** religion?

Miss Venus: No, Mrs. Brown, I love my religion very much. According to me, **religion is a way in which we express our gratitude to our creator, not asking or hoping to get something from him.** And I hates everything of Dr. A.

Ian Brown: But why that much hate from Dr. A.

Miss Venus: First reason my brother's death and second reason atrocities on poor people in this world! Maybe you don't see it but if the policies of Dr. A will not stopped then the dynasty of many people will end. Venus describes Ian about the condition of the common people. Ian Brown was shocked upon hearing Venus talk.

Ian Brown: So, what could we do, after knowing from you that Dr. A killed my father, I also wants to take revenge from him.

Miss Venus: We cannot do anything alone we have to gather many people with us, that too secretly from Dr. A.

Saying that Venus returns to her home.

CHAPTER SEVEN

BEGINNING OF REVOLUTION

Mrs. Brown was old. That's why she could not remember things and she still considered Dr. A to be a good person. But Ian Brown was very impressed by what Venus had said and wanted to take revenge on Dr. A. He had told this thing to Venus many times as well.

Due to the closure of the SSO by Dr. A, many families had stopped getting compensation for the death of their relatives. Because of this, now the deposited capital of Venus was also slowly getting depleted. And poor people were dying of starvation and diseases. Venus could not stand watching it . She knew that if nothing is done about Dr. A soon, then people of the poor population of the world could die. Miss Venus tells Ian Brown about all these things.

Miss Venus: We don't have much time left, now we have to take some concrete steps as soon as possible. Otherwise, millions of people will die in poverty, starvation and Dr. A's experiments.

Ian Brown: We have to start the fight against Doctor A by bringing all these people together.

Miss Venus: No, we can't do that, because these people doesn't have enough power to fight against Dr. A.

Ian Brown: So, what can we do?

Miss Venus: I have gathered information that Dr. A had occupied many countries by force, and after that these people surrendered themselves in front of Dr. A.

Ian Brown: But, now these people are with Dr. A

Miss Venus: Even though they are with Doctor A now, they want to regain their former position and maybe, they will join us in this fight against Doctor A.

Ian Brown: But, how do we reach them?

Miss Venus: First of all we have to create a revolution brigade of ours, and we will have to do ostentatious attacks on some of Dr. A's locations.

Ian Brown: But, why that?

Miss Venus: So that news can reach to those people that some revolutionary organization has started a fight against Dr. A, so that they will come themselves in search of us and offer to support us.

Ian Brown: But you said, that these people doesn't have the power to fight Dr. A.

Miss Venus: I told the truth but it would only be a ostentatious attack just to get people's attention.

Ian Brown was only questioning till now, which makes Venus a little suspicious of him, and she ends it by saying that, but even this ostentatious attack would require a lot of money which is not on me.

Ian Brown didn't gave any response. Venus returns to her home, And worries about how to raise so much money. A few days later, Ian Brown's call comes on Venus.

Ian Brown: Venus, money has been arranged. Now we can start our fight against Doctor A. Venus becomes very happy.

Venus: Thank you Mr. Ian, but still we have to gather people for our this fight.

After this, Ian Brown and Venus themselves roamed around and gathered people who wanted to free the world from Doctor A and also wanted to end **"The Divine Touch"**. Within a month, about 80 people had joined, most of whom were over the age of 40, whose children had died because of **"The Divine Touch"**.

Weapons were raised for the people of this brigade with the money raised by Ian Brown. So that the first gimmicky attack can be carried out according to the plan. And some ex-servicemen also joined them. In preparation for all these things, Venus tells Ian.

Venus: Mr. Ian, we have to think a name for our brigade, so people could easily identify us.

Ian Brown: Yes, name is mandatory, do you have any suggestions?

Venus: It all started with the deaths of my brother and your father, so according to me our brigade's name should be **L.B.** LB means Lawrence and Brown.

Ian Brown: Wouldn't it be awkward to name that in front of the world.

Venus: No Mr. Ian, this thing will stay just between us, that LB (Lawrence, Brown). And for the rest of the world the meaning of **LB** will be **Liberation Brigade.**

Ian Brown: This suggestion will be fine, It can also act as our password when needed.

Venus: (laughing out loud) Mr. Ian you are talking exactly like detective movies.

In this one month Venus and Ian Brown became very frank with each other. The site of the attack is fixed in a building, which was under construction , in which a new hall of **'The Trust'** was to be built. The night time was chosen for the attack so that no worker would be threatened in this attack, the building was demolished by a total of 8 people of the brigade by bombing and later **LB** took the responsibility through the internet.

This new spread like fire, that an organization named **LB** has come in revolt of Dr. A. But Dr. A did not responded to it. Due to this news, many big people have become alert. These were the people who were compulsively supporting Dr. A. They also wanted to get rid of the Dr. A. They had started to find out about **LB**.

On the other hand Venus and other members of **LB** were celebrating their first victory.

IanBrown: Venus, we are getting many people's invitations. They wants to meet is once, so they could join us in this war against Dr. A.

Venus: But Mr. Ian, we have to stay cautious, It may also happen that some of these people are with Dr. A and are doing this to trap us, so for the time being we will meet those selected people. Those whom we already have news that they are really against Dr. A.

Ian Brown: You are right.

Venus: If you remember, that before some time many countries made an alliance against Dr. A, we have to meet these people.

Venus organizes a meeting with representatives of all those former countries. The meeting takes place at an intelligence site in which representatives of the countries and Venus and Ian Brown take part. Delegates from all countries welcome Ian Brown as the head of the **LB**.

Mr. Carter: (While pointing at Venus) Mr. Ian why did you bring this kid along with you in such an intelligence meeting.

Ian Brown: Mr. Brown, actually she is the head of our brigade, her name is Miss Venus.

Mr. Richard: (Fiercely) Is there a joke going on here? Do you not know that if Dr. A has defeated the big countries of the world, then what will this girl do?

Miss Merry: We find out that Doctor A started researching **"The Divine Touch"** 19 years ago. At that time this girl would not have even been born.

Venus: (Loudly) It's not right to guess someone's capabilities by their age, hardly any of you would know more about Dr. A than me. Dr. A has taken my brother from me. No one can hate Dr. A more than me. All of you people must have started investigation about Dr. A from two-three years ago but I am doing this from 5 years ago.

Ian Brown: (Pacifying Venus) Venus is right, attack on Dr. A's location, gathering peoples for brigade and fixing meeting with all of you were all Venus's strategy. Even though Venus is young, she is a very talented and intelligent girl.

Everyone calms down after listening to Ian and apologizes to Venus. The meeting continues.

Mr. Carter: We are ready to support your brigade.

Miss Merry: But, we can only support you with money and weapons, we can not join you in a direct manner.

Mr. Richard: You are right, because once we have faced the consequences by going against Dr. A. If we do this again, our lives will be in danger.

Venus: That would be enough, all of you thanks a lot.

The meeting ends and everyone returns. The weapons and money are delivered to the **LB**. Coming back to her home, Venus talks to Ian Brown.

Venus: Mr. Ian thanks for supporting me in front of representatives.

Ian Brown: You don't have to thank me. I just told them truth.

Venus: I have been living alone since the death of my brother and mother, and no one was with me.

Ian Brown: Don't worry, now me and my mother are with you, think of us as your family. Saying that Ian Brown embraces Venus.

Weapons were given to the brigade's members from the next day, and there training started, arrangements of this training were done by former countries. Venus and Ian Brown recruits new members in their brigade. Because now they had more than enough money, so they helped many poor peoples with it. Now the Liberation Brigade has a total of 400 members and the training of all of them lasts for 3 months. Venus and Ian Brown talk to each other to prepare for a new attack after training ends.

Ian Brown: Venus, have you decided about the new location for attack.

Venus: Yes Mr. Ian, but it would not be a attack, but a rescue mission.

Ian Brown: Rescue mission, but how?

Venus: See, at this place there is a laboratory of Dr. A, in which many people are held captive for the use of **"The Divine Touch"**, In which there are people of all ages, young and old. So we will attack this lab and rescue them all from there.

Ian Brown: When will we do this attack?

Venus: Tonight, because it could be fatal for them, to spend even one day there.

Ian Brown: (Uncomfortably) But tonight will be very early, our soldiers will not be able to prepare.

Venus: Do you have any problem with it.

Ian Brown: No, as you think is right.

At night time, Venus with almost 20 soldiers, frees those people by attacking on laboratory, these people were very frightened, because they knew that they were going to be used in the operations of **"The Divine Touch"**. After getting freed from laboratory, all people gave thanks to Venus and other soldiers of **LB**. Some of those people returned to their homes, while others requested Venus for joining **LB**.

There was also a 12 years old boy in the captives, who had not yet returned home. Venus saw that the little boy had not yet gone home and was sitting alone in a corner. Venus goes to that boy.

Venus: Boy, what's your name? Why haven't you gone to your house yet?

Little Boy: (Eerily) My name is Andrew, thank you for saving me.

Venus: So Andrew, why haven't you gone to your house yet? Shall I take you to your parents?

Andrew: (Sadly) My parents are no more, I am alone, please don't get me out from here.

After listening Andrew's words, Venus remember her past, that how she also used to live alone. But Venus had compensation money, and Andrew didn't even had that.

Venus: Don't afraid, no one will get you out, from today you can think of me as your older sister, my name is Venus. From today you will live with us.

After listening that Andrew became happy, and again thanked Venus.

Venus: Andrew, how did your parents died.

Andrew: Before some time my father was forcibly caught by Dr. A's people, then he didn't returned, after that my mother died from illness. And one day when I went after Dr. A's people for searching my father, then they caught me as well. After knowing that Venus's hate for Dr. A increased.

Andrew: Elder sister, include me in your brigade as well. I also wants to take my parent's revenge from Dr. A.

Andrew also had the same feeling, which came into Venus's mind before 5 years, but Venus knew that their path was very dangerous and Andrew was still too young, Venus said to Andrew that,

Venus: Andrew, you are too young right now, so leave Dr. A on us. And for now go with them. Saying that Venus sent Andrew to a refugee camp**Venus:** Having said this, Venus sends Andrew to a refugee camp where women, children and old people lived and their expenses were met by **LB**.

Andrew: (While going) Elder sister, will you come to meet me again?

Venus: (Smiling) Yes sure, take care of yourself Andrew.

The news of the attack on Doctor A's laboratory spreads all over the world. After hearing **LB's** name in this too, everyone starts seeing **LB** as a powerful organization, but Doctor A does not react to this either.

As **LB's** popularity grows, many people raise their hands to support them. Also many people start coming to join the **Liberation Brigade**. But still, Venus neither accepts the help of any rich person nor includes anyone in the organization without investigation.

CHAPTER EIGHT

SUPPRESSION

Gradually **LB** has more than 2000 members, and now their training also starts. Meanwhile, Venus gets a call from Mr. Carter. He invites Venus to visit. Venus reaches there with Mr. Ian on the fixed time.

Mr. Carter: Hello, Miss Venus, today I invited you for a very important matter.

Miss Venus: Tell, Mr. Carter.

Mr. Carter: Miss Venus, watching growing power of your brigade, many people wants to support you.

Ian Brown: Who are these people? Mr. Carter.

Mr. Carter: Pardon me Mr. Ian, but I cannot tell you about them.

Miss Venus: But, why?

Mr. Carter: Because they have set a condition, that they will help you in every way, but won't expose their identity.

Ian Brown: But, why won't they expose their identity?

Mr. Carter: In these people, all powerful personalities which are against Dr. A are included. But they don't wants to risk their lives by exposing their identities.

Miss Venus: Can we trust them?

Mr. Carter: I takes responsibility. These people's words are that if **LB** defeats Dr. A, then they will expose their identities in front of everyone.

Miss Venus: (Fiercely) What do they thinks? That we are their hired goons. Which will fight for them, this fight is to avenge this world, not for taking some bigwigs revenge.

Mr.Carter: Calm down Miss Venus, these people can help you a lot.

Ian Brown: (Explaining Venus) Venus, our brigade is increasing, and for managing that big organization, we will need more money otherwise our brigade will fall apart. And this fight will remain incomplete, for that we have to accept their help, for now we have to forget emotions and bring this fight to its goal.

Venus knew that only a little time was left, That's why she accepts Mr. Carter's offer even though she doesn't want to. After that **Liberation Brigade's** power increased more. They attacked Dr. A's different laboratories and free several captives. They also damaged much of Dr. A's property. A ray of hope wakes up in the minds of poor people around the world, that at last someone has come to save us from the atrocities of Dr. A. The name of Venus and **Liberation Brigade** becomes very famous all over the world. Everyone looks to Venus as their 'savior'.

Even after all this has happened, Dr. A does not take any action against the **Liberation Brigade**. Due to which a little doubt arises in the mind of Venus. That what is the reason behind Doctor A's calmness. Venus was thinking about it during the night, so Ian Brown, who were sleeping near her, wakes up. Venus and Ian Brown had become very close while living together since the beginning of the **Liberation Brigade**. They had decided that after the end of this fight, both would get married.

Ian Brown: Venus, what are you thinking this much late night.

Venus: Ian I'm thinking, that even after happening that much, why is not Dr. A reacting.

Ian Brown: Maybe he is thinking us weak, that **LB** is not a big threat.

Venus: If we look closely, we have not done much damage to Dr. A in all the attacks so far. Except in the one where we saved Andrew, and it seems as though Dr. A knows about every attack in advance, and is intentionally letting us win easily.

Ian Brown: Don't think that much, tomorrow is your 19th birthday, have some rest and sleep. Saying that Ian embraced Venus and both slept.

Next day, Venus says to Ian Brown.

Venus: Ian, which thing I said last night, we have to think about that.

Ian Brown: Do you thinks that there is a spy in our brigade?

Venus: By the way, I had recruited all the people after conducting my own investigation. But Doctor A may have bought one of these.

Ian Brown: But, how will we find out that?

Venus: For now, Finding this out would be hard, so to be cautious,. From today all the plans will be between you and me. The plans will be communicated to the members of the brigade only 1 hour in advance. I can't trust anyone more than you.

Ian Brown: This will be right. By the way let's celebrate your birthday today.

Venus: No Ian, I haven't celebrated my birthday from many years, because I had decided that until I save this world from Dr. A, I will not celebrate anything. This fight started with the revenge of my brother's death, but now after watching the situation of poor peoples, I wants to fight for them.

Ian Brown: (Watching Venus's serious face) At least don't speak this seriously on your birthday.

So, on Venus, Mr. Carter's message arrives. He invites Venus and Ian to meet. Venus and Ian Brown arrive at the designated place and talk to Mr. Carter.

Venus: Mr. Carter, why has you called us today?

Mr. Carter: Miss Venus, I have a message for you.

Ian Brown: Message! But from who?

Mr. Carter: From 'The Saviors' .

Miss Venus: 'The Saviors' but who are they? Is this a new organization which has stood against Dr. A.

Mr. Carter: 'The Saviors' are the same people who are finding you, they has named their group 'The Saviors'.

Venus: (Fiercely) What are these people doing except funding us? They are only cowards, which can't even tell their identities. Above all the big name 'The Saviors', why are they acting as they are fighting Doctor A with their lives at stake, they are only hungry for credit.

Ian Brown: (While calming down Venus) So tell Mr. Carter, what's their message.

Mr. Carter: They says that, they wants to get rid of Dr. A as soon as possible, so their order is, that you have to attack on Dr. A's location soon.

Miss Venus: (Angrily) What did you said? Order! We are not their slaves, they are funding us because we have same motive, our brigade won't take orders from anyone. We will do our work in our way.

Mr. Carter: Don't get angry, I'm just telling you their words.

Ian Brown: So, tell them too, we are not their servants, which they will command.

Ian Brown calmed down Venus.

Ian Brown: Tell me what else they have to say?

Mr. Carter: They wants you to attack Dr. A with your whole brigade.

Miss Venus: Do your 'The Saviors' have bundles of notes instead of brains in their head? If we do this, Doctor A will wipe out all our brigade with the help of 'The Dark Savior' and we will lose this battle.

Mr. Carter: So, when will you attack Dr. A.

Miss Venus: Will do soon, but for now we can only fight in small groups, this too in guerilla warfare. Because **The Dark Savior** can't be used in small areas. Mr. Carter I'm not against rich peoples, but I hate those people who, even in such a situation, are more concerned about their position, reputation than the lives of other people, those who think that they are superior.

Mr. Carter: I understands Miss Venus, and I will also make them understand. Your brigade is the hope of this world.

After that Ian Brown and Venus returned and start making upcoming plans.

On the other hand Dr. A was talking with Hopkin.

Dr. A: Hopkin, now time has come to answer **Liberation Brigade**, we have to use those two brothers.

Hopkin: All right, I will make the arrangements.

(Which two brothers, Dr. A was talking about, it was a mystery).

In **LB** Venus tells Ian Brown about the next plan.

Venus: It is true that now we have to plan the preparations for the attack on Dr. A because now there is very little time left.

Ian Brown: You are right, we have to do something soon.

Venus: Dr. A is coming to this city after 2 days, we have to execute this attack on the same day, because Dr. A's personal army will be with him, so we have to execute this attack in night.

Ian Brown: But our brigade will not be able to face them even in night, because their numbers are too large.

Venus: For that we have to split our brigade in two squads, for which the first squad will attack at the building of **The Trust** nearby Dr. A's accommodation. So that Dr. A's attention will go towards that attack, and he will send his army to that place, then there will be fewer soldiers under the protection of Dr. A. After that another squad will go to attack the Dr. A.

Ian Brown: What if Dr. A fled after hearing about the attack?

Venus: This will not happen, because we will place our soldiers on the rooftops of surrounding buildings, so no helicopter can go from there.

Ian Brown: You made whole plan by yourself, well done Venus!

Venus: First squad of our brigade, which will attack **The Trust's** building will be led by you, and I will lead the second squad.

Ian Brown: It's all fine, but why in night?

Venus: Because in the day time, there will be common people around that building, so for their security and in night our brigade will easily be able to do gorilla warfare. And remember that first squad's motive is to keep Dr. A's army entangled, not defeating them. Because it can be dangerous. And if the other group succeeds, Dr. A's forces will themselves give up.

Mr. Carter and 'The saviors' gets told about this plan, Mr. Carter supplied more weapons and material to

Liberation Brigade, also the entire Liberation brigade was put into more rigorous training and another squad was added to the plan.

Eventually Dr. A comes to the city, **Liberation Brigade,** gets divided into 3 squads, first which will be led by Ian Brown (900 members), second squad which will be led by Venus (800) members, and third squad which was to monitor over buildings rooftops. Rest 200 members were left for the security of their base. At night, the first squad which was led by Ian Brown attacks **The Trust's** building, after getting the news of attack, Dr. A sent his all soldiers there, and only kept 2 soldiers for his security.

Ian and his group begin a conflict with Dr. A's personal army, and upon hearing this, Venus directs the third squad, sending the second squad to attack Dr. A's residence.

When second squad reached at that place , they only saw 2 soldiers there, which were not wearing any kind of safety gadgets and there faces were covered, and they had laser weapons, protection from which protection was impossible with a common safety jacket.

Yet the soldiers of the second squad were much more in numbers than them, and they were only 2, so the attack begins. One by one the soldiers of the second squad started falling. After a while they realize that their bullets were not having any effect on these two soldiers, but bullets were coming back after hitting them. On knowing this, there was a stampede in the second squad , and those two soldiers of Dr. A started killing everyone by catching them.

The soldier of the second squad went and told all this to Venus. On listening to the soldier, Venus understood what was the matter, Venus told the soldier that,

Venus: Almost before 9 years, the scientists of King White's country had 2 successes in DNA modification, which they refused to expose to the world, but after King White's death, Dr. A occupied his country, with it he also included these two persons in his private army. We also received an information from 'The Saviors' that there are also two brothers in Dr. A's private army, which were made by modifying DNA with an animal named **Armadillo**. Sure, they both are same.

Soldier: But Miss Venus, Both of them have killed 200 of our soldiers so far.

Venus: Bullets will not affect those two, so tell other soldiers to retreat.

The soldiers of the second group retreat and Venus herself goes with her special squad. By now 350 soldiers of the second detachment had died. Seeing the dead bodies of his soldiers everywhere, Venus feels very sad. Also she gets angry.

On the other hand, Doctor A's army was overshadowing Ian's squad, because Dr. A's army had a thousand soldiers. At the same time, 1500 local security force soldiers were also joined by them, due to which 80 soldiers of the first squad had died so far, and 130 soldiers of Dr. A's army.

Venus reached in front of those two soldiers with her special squad. Seeing Venus, they talk to each other.

Walter: Big brother, see, This is the same girl whose photo was shown by Dr. A. V......ve......

Flint: Venus!

Walter: Yes Venus. If we catch her, Dr. A will set us free then we can go back home.

Flint: Don't speak rubbish, Walter. Now there is no home left to go back to. After saying this, both of them run towards Venus to attack.

But before they come close, Venus and her special squad start bombarding them. One after another blasts, both of them get badly injured. After which Venus sees that the skin of both of them was very hard, which was now crumpled like a shield. Both of them were then killed, and Venus goes inside the building to find Dr. A.

Walking around the building, Venus sees Dr. A. He was wearing protective equipment. Venus and his companions chase Dr. A, various traps were laid in the building to protect Dr. A, 6 soldiers died in these traps chasing Dr. A, so to avoid these traps, Venus thrown a bomb on Dr. A from distance, and Dr. A gets injured, before Venus could have spoke. Soldiers of the special squad captured Dr. A and killed him and started celebrating their victory.

The news of Dr. A's death was spread, and also the news of victory of the Liberation Brigade. Upon receiving this news, there was no reason to continue the war on Dr. A's personal army, as they were compulsively supporting Dr. A. With this the war ends. Medical facilities are being taken to the injured. However, Hopkin and **"The Divine Touch"** had not yet found.

People from whole world started celebrating the victory of **Liberation Brigade**, But the Liberation Brigade first pays tribute to its martyred soldiers. A total of 436 soldiers of the Liberation Brigade had died in the war against Dr. A.

Mr. Carter and **The Saviors** congratulates Venus and the Liberation Brigade on their victory. The next day, a ceremony was organized by **The Saviors,** in which all those who have directly or indirectly participated in this fight against Dr. A were present. However, Venus refuses to attend the ceremony because she knew, that **The Saviors** just wanted to get all the credit via this ceremony.

All the soldiers of **Liberation Brigade** were also present in this ceremony except Venus and Ian Brown. Although, for security reasons normal peoples were not allowed in this ceremony, but it's broadcast was live all over the world. The members of **The Saviors** exaggeratedly praise themselves, that we have given all the instructions to the **Liberation Brigade**, made plans, and present themselves as the new democratic rulers of the world. People all over the world were watching this broadcast.

On the other hand, Venus was watching this broadcast with Ian Brown, She gets very angry hearing The Saviors, and she turns off the TV.

Ian Brown: Venus cool down your head, I will get you the juice.

Venus: (While drinking juice) Ian, now we've saved the world from Dr. A, so now we both shall marry.

Ian Brown: We both will marry exactly tomorrow.

Venus: (Happily) Finally, people's lives will be happy again and ours too.

While the ceremony of **The Saviors** was going on, suddenly a missile hits the venue, killing everyone present in the blast. The broadcast of the function stops. Shortly after this, there is a gathering of media people, and news of this blast starts coming on all the channels. Those who were just celebrating their independence. 'Fear strikes again in their minds'.

Ian Brown turns on the television, On seeing the news of this missile attack, Venus drowns in serious concern. She could not understand, who could be behind this attack. Dr. A had died, so who was the one who would attack Doctor A's enemies? Thinking so, Venus suddenly faints.

When Venus regained consciousness, she was in an unknown place, and her hands and feet were tied. A man was sitting in front of Venus.

That Man: (Taunting) Good morning, Venus.

Venus: You are Mr. Emerald, To whom Dr. A had given the responsibility of the third continent. Was that attack also done by you, why are you doing this, now that Dr. A has died, now you do not need to do this under compulsion.

That Man: Calm down Venus, undoubtedly this body is of Mr. Emerald, but (while pointing at his brain), do you knows who is here?

Venus: This can't be true, how could this happen?

That Man: (Laughing loudly) You guessed right, I'm Dr. A.

Venus: But we had killed you, was he someone else?

Dr. A: The one you killed was also me. Even though you are my enemy but you entertained me so much, so I will tell you all the truth.

After this Dr. A starts telling everything to Venus.

Dr. A: People thinks that **"The Divine Touch"** transfers memories from one brain to another, but it's only half truth, nobody knows about the real power of **"The Divine Touch"**. It can collect memory from a person's brain, which we can copy in infinite bodies or say brains, from the beginning I never trusted anyone except Hopkin, so all the people who are ruling all continents. **All of them are me.**

Venus: (Interrupting Dr. A) Where is Ian, what did you do with him?

Dr. A: (Laughing) What do you thinks, that how you reached here? Remember what you drank before fainting.

By this time Ian comes there.

Venus: Ian free me, this person is Dr. A.

Ian Brown: Not Ian, my name is Hopkin.

Hearing this, Venus fills with tears. She had always relied on Ian Brown the most and was now in shock after she lost her trust.

Dr. A: We always feared, that maybe in the future, someone will go to you or Mrs. Brown to find out about us. So when Mrs. Brown came to us for treatment with Ian, we copied Hopkin's memory into his brain because I only had trust over Hopkin. Till date we have eliminated all the people who came to Mrs. Brown. Only left you because you were a kid, but I told Hopkin to win your trust. I used to get all your plans from Hopkin in advance.

Venus: (While wiping her tears) If that was the case, then why did you pretended your death?

Dr. A: Because I knew, that some people will not expose their identities until they confirms my death. And by the way, **Gods doesn't dies by one death.** Saying that Dr. A started laughing loudly.

Venus felt like, that until now she was a puppet of Dr. A's hands.

Dr. A: By using you I have eliminated all my direct and indirect enemies at once. Now this world will be like that again. Your struggle was in vain.

All hopes of Venus was finished, And she also felt the shock of losing her trust.

Dr. A: **"Normal humans can't defeat gods"**, Venus, you eliminated my one body, **I'm not one but many.** Venus was waiting for her death sitting silently.

Dr. A: Hopkin, what did she said to you?

Hopkin: That, finally people's lives will be happy again and ours too.

Dr. A: (Loudly) This is not a movie, which will have a happy ending.

Dr. A: (In serious tone) **Real life doesn't have happy endings.** Saying this, Dr. A shoots Venus.

***END*

(Source: writer's imagination)

www.ingramcontent.com/pod-product-compliance
Lightning Source LLC
Chambersburg PA
CBHW031418160726
47993CB00003B/1297